HIDDEN WONDERS!

HIDDEN WONDERS!

A CAN YOU SEE WHAT I SEE? BOOK

by

WALTER WICK

CARTWHEEL BOOKS

An Imprint of Scholastic Inc.

FOR LINDA

TABLE OF CONTENTS

MAKEUP MASQUERADE

*Can you see
what I see?*

A mouse, a monkey,
and two bow ties,
a tiger, 3 turtles,
4 butterflies;

a zebra mask,
sunglasses, too,
a golden feather,
a button that's blue;

a lizard, a lion,
a crown for a king,
a diamond saber,
and a ruby ring!

MIRROR MAGIC

*Can you see
what I see?*

A fish, a fisherman,
5 funny clowns,
3 airplanes,
2 royal crowns;

a pig, a calf,
an Earth, a moon,
a red ladybug,
a hot air balloon;

10 fun dominoes,
9 tricky dice —
careful not to count
the same ones twice!

WHIRLING WONDERS

*Can you see
what I see?*

A twirling dancer,
a break in a string,
wind-up teeth,
2 wagons, a spring;

a strawberry top,
2 horses, 2 mice,
a soccer player,
a baseball, 4 dice;

a bunny, 2 carrots,
a duck's yellow bill —
match 6 spinning tops
with 6 that are still!

FLATLAND

*Can you see
what I see?*

2 letter X's,
a bear, a moose,
a tiger, 6 trees,
a swan, a goose;

a red umbrella,
a blue crayon tip,
a pig, a parrot,
a pink paper clip;

a little blue chair,
a clothespin, 2 clocks,
a flower, and 3 large
flat paper blocks!

THE WIZARD'S MIRROR

*Can you see
what I see?*

2 dragon wings,
a brass arrowhead,
a paintbrush, a pen,
a spool of thread;

3 scorpions,
a serpent, a snail,
a feather, 3 frogs,
a raccoon's tail;

2 hourglasses,
a gold dragon frame,
a snuffed-out candle,
and its still-burning flame!

COSTUME BALL

*Can you see
what I see?*

A pretty cat costume,
a carriage wheel,
a butterfly mask,
a sword of steel;

a rabbit, a robot,
a pirate's hook,
musical notes,
and Bo-Peep's crook;

a gentleman peacock,
a witch's broom,
and 31 partygoers
in one mirrored room!

RECYCLED ROBOTS

*Can you see
what I see?*

2 hand mixers,
a magnet, a star,
a microphone,
a cell phone, a car;

5 paper clips,
a hammer, a chain,
a fish, an owl,
a peanut, a plane;

7 spoons, a saw,
a hydrant, 5 hearts,
and 4 robots made
from recycled parts!

MAGIC DRAGON

*Can you see
what I see?*

A watermelon slice,
a bucket that's blue,
an ice cream cone,
a green turtle, too;

a button, a fishhook,
a pretty pearl ring,
a bent bottle cap,
a straw and a string;

3 feathers, 5 birds,
a sand-filled wagon,
2 horsemen, an archer,
and a magic sand dragon!

GAME BOARD ILLUSION

*Can you see
what I see?*

4 bees, 3 birds,
2 buttons, 2 bears,
a red strawberry,
a shovel, 3 chairs;

a lion, a mouse,
a curvy kite tail,
a trick elephant,
an upside-down pail;

an apple, a pear,
a little barn door,
and 4 painted blocks
that blend with the floor!

CABINET OF CURIOSITIES

*Can you see
what I see?*

A queen of hearts,
a barefoot king,
a microscope,
a bell to ring;

3 wise owls,
a curious dog,
a bat skeleton,
a musical frog;

a horse and rider,
red lava flow,
and a reflected
rabbit on the go!

Cutting a Thread Hung in a Bottle.

WACKY WORKSHOP

*Can you see
what I see?*

5 elephants,
a long cat tail,
a spool, a broom,
a bent brass nail;

4 smokestacks,
a wooden clothespin,
a pig, a pony,
a toy top to spin;

endless stairs,
2 shoelaces,
and a house that's
impossible
in 3 different places!

SPACE STATION IMPOSSIBLE

*Can you see
what I see?*

A camera, 2 clocks,
2 keys for a car,
5 steps to a plane,
an electric guitar;

a harp, a magnet,
a man in the moon,
a grater for cheese,
a fork, knife, and spoon;

a purple bracelet,
a mirror and a comb,
and 3 friends in
a spaceship
headed for home!

ABOUT THIS BOOK

I'm not sure when the wonder and fascination with optical illusions first took hold in my brain. Perhaps it started at a very young age when I became entranced, Alice-like, with that elusive world beyond the mirror: a world just like the "real" one, only backward and forever out of reach. Later, I encountered "impossible object" illusions — drawings of three-dimensional objects that defy logic — such as the Penrose triangle, impossibly joined by three right-angle corners, or Escher stairs, which appear to ascend endlessly in a continuous loop. Over the years I've incorporated such illusions into my photo illustrations from time to time, culminating in a book devoted to the subject, *Walter Wick's Optical Tricks* (Cartwheel Books, 1998). The book you now hold, *Hidden Wonders*, blends these visual wonders with the search-and-find game for the first time. In doing so, I hope to tap into my readers' typically intensive scrutiny of the visual realm and take them beyond the mirror — and into the wondrous, magical realm of visual illusions.

Longtime readers of the Can You See What I See? series may notice that Seymour has acquired a new friend named Buttons — a faithful dog who accompanies Seymour on all his adventures. And for this title, the pair have met up with a cat named Lucky. Lucky is a "waving cat," a symbol of good luck in Japan, and is included here as a special thank-you to my legions of Japanese readers, who are among the biggest Can You See What I See? fans outside the United States.

ACKNOWLEDGMENTS

I'd like to thank the following people who helped make this book possible: my editor, Kyoko Kiire, at Shogakukan, Japan, for her steady support and encouragement; Shigesato Itoi for his delightful translations from English to Japanese; my agent, Maiko Fujinaga, at Japan Uni, for her expert guidance. For this US edition, thanks go to editor Ken Geist, art director Brian LaRossa, and the entire team at Scholastic who made this edition possible. At the studio, very special thanks go to my studio assistant, Heather Aylsworth, whose artistic skills and prop-making talents blossomed during the making of this book, resulting in invaluable contributions of numerous details small and large; to Randy Gilman, who sculpted many of the custom figures for "Costume Ball" as well as the dragon frame in "The Wizard's Mirror." Finally, I'm deeply indebted to my wife, Linda, for her unfailing support and artistic wisdom, without which this book would not be possible.

Walter Wick

ABOUT THE AUTHOR

Walter Wick is the author and photographer of *A Ray of Light* and *A Drop of Water*. He is also the creator of the internationally bestselling Can You See What I See? series as well as the photographer of the highly acclaimed I Spy series, with riddles by Jean Marzollo. He has created photographs for books, magazines, and newspapers including the *New York Times* and *Newsweek*. Walter's photographs have been featured in museums throughout the United States. He lives with his wife, Linda, in Miami, Florida.

More information about Walter Wick is available at walterwick.com.